Get a glimpse of
Incredible Journey Book Four

IN PARADISE

and all of the other
Incredible Journey Books

By going to . . .
www.IJBOOKS.com

Join the I.J. Club
while you're there!

Dear kids:

I'm so glad you decided to join Max and Sam on their adventure to Africa. You're in for a fun ride (no pun intended)!

You're going to learn so much about the animals of Africa and why the phrase "it's a jungle out there" is used so often. As you will find out, the jungle is a scary place . . . a place you must be on guard at all times. There is always an animal predator just around the corner . . . watching . . . and waiting . . . for its next victim.

Oh, enough about that. I don't want to scare you off before the tale begins.

So . . . (drum roll, please) let the adventure begin. . . .

P.S. Have a great time and remember to always keep your imagination alive!

An Incredible Journey Book

# ADVENTURE
# IN AFRICA

Book
Three

# by Connie Lee Berry

This book is dedicated to Sydney and to all of her friends in kindergarten. . . . Your adventure in learning has just begun!

Mrs. White's kindergarten class:

Marc
Sydney
Luca
Alberto
Michael
Derek
Ean
Alex
Sean
Addison

Thanks, Matt . . . for all of your help.

ISBN 10: 0977284824
ISBN 13: 9780977284825
This book is part of the Incredible Journey Books series.

Text copyright© 2007 by Connie Lee Berry.
All rights reserved. Published by Kid's Fun Press in 2007.

Printed in the U.S.A.

# TABLE OF CONTENTS

1. Invisible Ink
2. The Cleanup
3. Zoology Camp
4. Africa Bound
5. The Perky Lady
6. Campout
7. Spot the Animals
8. Charger
9. Cries in the Jungle

# Fun facts about Africa . . .

**A** mazing animals—Africa is home to four out of five of the fastest land animals: the cheetah, wildebeest, lion, and gazelle.

**F** orests—Make up 25% of Africa. Rainforests are found in its Congo river basin.

**R** ivers and lakes—Africa is home to the Nile, the world's longest river, and Lake Victoria, the world's second-largest lake.

**I** nsects—Africa is home to some unusual insects including the goliath beetle, the world's largest and heaviest beetle, and the dwarf blue butterfly, the world's smallest butterfly.

**C** entral location—Africa is the most centrally located continent in the world and is almost cut equally in half by the equator.

**A** tlantic Ocean—This ocean stretches to the west of Africa.

# Other facts about Africa . . .

Africa is the second-largest continent in the world, covering about 20% of the world's land area.

Africa is divided into over 50 countries, including its islands, and has around 1000 spoken languages.

The world's oldest desert, the Namib, and the world's largest desert, the Sahara, are located in Africa.

Africa produces a large supply of the world's diamonds and gold, but is still the poorest continent. Up until 2007, the world's largest gem-quality diamond was the Cullinan, which was found in South Africa in 1905 and weighed 3,106 carats uncut. Some of the British crown jewels came from this diamond when it was cut. In 2007, a diamond was found in South Africa that weighed 7,000 carats!

Africa is home to the island of Madagascar, which has the world's smallest as well as the world's largest chameleons.

# Prologue

In the first *Incredible Journey Book*, *The Criminal in the Caymans*, two mysterious boxes arrived on Max and Sam's doorstep. In one box, they found an old leather journal. Inside the journal was yellowed paper with a note scribbled on the first page that said, "Notes taken wisely can be of great use to you." In the second box, they found a map dated October 11, 1964 and labeled "Max and Sam's Incredible Journey Map."

Since that time, a new letter has mysteriously appeared on the map with each trip they take. In the Cayman Islands, a "W" appeared. In Tahiti, an "I" appeared.

Max and Sam have not discovered who sent the map or the journal or why the letters keep appearing on the map. These mysteries will be solved in one of the later *Incredible Journey Books*.

## Chapter One
# INVISIBLE INK

S am felt a quick tinge of pain. "Ouch!" he
shouted, while rubbing his arm.

He spun around. He stared at the girls seated at the table behind him to see if one of them could be the source of his pain.

*No*, he decided. Raegan, Katie, Hannah, and Audrey looked preoccupied with working on their projects.

Sam whirled back around and caught the eye of the boy sitting next to him in summer camp.

"Sorry," Colin said with a slight mischievous gleam in his eye. "Didn't mean to pinch you so hard. I just noticed you were about to drift off to sleep."

"Don't let it happen again," Sam warned playfully. "Or else—"

"Want to help us pull a prank on Mrs. McLean?" Ryan said, appearing suddenly between their chairs. "Timmy has a great idea, and the worst thing that could happen is that we get kicked out of summer camp."

"Maybe that's not such a bad idea. Doing crafts all day isn't my kind of fun," a girl sitting at the table said, staring down at her messy shell photo-frame project. The girl, named Allicea, laughed and held up three of her fingers that were stuck together with glue.

"I don't know," Sam said, reluctant to do anything that might keep him from going to zoology camp. "We start studying animals tomorrow—Raegan's dad is an animal trainer at the zoo, and he's volunteered to teach us."

That mischievous look returned to Colin's

eye. "And you're going to need lots of training on your trip to Africa, with all those wild beasts on the move, prowling around looking for fresh, juicy meat to—"

"Chomp all the life out of you!" Laci blurted out, after popping in to eavesdrop. She made a sarcastic chuckle and rushed off again upon hearing a roar of laughter at the end of the room.

"Did I hear something about a prank?" Dillon said, casually walking up and sitting down at Sam and Colin's table.

"Yeah, Timmy thought of one, and we thought we might get in on it," Colin said.

"*We?*" Sam said defensively. "I'm not so sure about it. Max will never forgive us if we get zoology camp cancelled."

"Oh, come on, Sam," Colin said. "Don't be such a wimp. And where is Max today anyway?"

"He's home with a cold," Sam mumbled. "And what did you call me—a *wimp*?" Sam said, as his eyes flared with anger. "Would a wimp go to Africa and camp out among all of those wild, meat-loving animals? I don't think so."

Sam glared at Colin, crossing his arms in front of him. Then he added defiantly, "A little prank would be *nothing* compared to that."

The laughter at the end of the room suddenly erupted again. "Come on then," Colin said, as he, Ryan, and Dillon got up and rushed across the room to see what was going on.

Sam sat there for a moment, thinking about how zoology camp would really come in handy before their trip to Africa.

Suddenly, more laughter came from the end of the room. "What in the world are they doing down there?" Sam thought to himself, annoyed by the overpowering curiosity building up inside of him.

Sam looked at his watch. . . . Mrs. Benson wouldn't be back for at least fifteen more minutes. She had rushed to the nurse's office with Austin W., who had a wheezing fit during afternoon recess. They add the "W" after his first name to avoid getting him confused with the other Auston who spells his name differently.

Austin W. usually had an asthma attack at least twice a week, especially during summer camp when they were outside so much. The class didn't mind, though, because it always meant an unexpected break.

Sam couldn't fight the urge anymore. He got up and ran across the room, only to find Jordan writing on the wall, surrounded by onlookers.

Sam edged over to Colin. "What's going on?" he said.

Even though there was no sign of Mrs. Benson, Colin cautiously looked around to make sure and then leaned over to whisper in Sam's ear. "Gabriel brought some glow-in-the-dark, invisible ink from his magic kit, and we're taking turns writing scary messages to frighten Mrs. McLean, the night-time cleaning lady."

"What did *you* write?" Sam whispered back.

"By the time I got here, Timmy had started the message by writing that he needed help. Then Laci added that he needed help because he had been kidnapped. Then Auston S. added that he was being held in the school library. Then I added that a ransom note was written on the wall in the bathroom by the cafeteria."

Colin's face beamed. "Pretty clever, huh? All someone has to do is tell Mrs. Benson that he needs to go to the bathroom and quickly write the note while he's there."

"Yeah," Sam mumbled, lost in thought, imagining what the wall would look like in the dark. He chuckled at the imaginary sight.

Help! I need help!

I have been kidnapped.

I am being held in the library.

There is a ransom note on the wall of the bathroom by the —

Colin interrupted Sam's vision. "And Jordan is now finishing up the note by writing that the police shouldn't be notified or his life will be in danger."

"I guess it *is* a foolproof plan," Sam said, impressed. After all, you couldn't even see the ink in the daytime.

But then a thought occurred to Sam. "How do you know Mrs. McLean will even *see* the writing on the wall and read the note? She could turn on the light before she even notices the writing."

Colin's face lit up proudly. "I already checked it out. The wall with the writing on it is directly opposite from the door, and the light switch is several feet down from the door. So when she opens up the door, the writing will be the first thing she sees—it would be impossible to miss it."

"Do you think she'll call the police?" Sam said, still concerned about zoology camp.

"Quit worrying. It'll be funny. First, we'll send her on a wild goose chase around the school. She'll go to the bathroom to read the ransom note, which will send her to the wall outside the—" Colin paused to think of a good place to send her with easy access.

"Oh, I know," Colin blurted out. "We'll send her to the outside wall by the kitchen door. That way whoever writes the note in the bathroom can also write that note on the way back."

"Will that be the last note?" Sam asked, surprised by how easy it all seemed.

"No, we'll write one more," Colin said, thinking hard about the next location. "Got it," he finally said. "We'll send her to the wall outside the office of Mrs. Fuller, the P.E. coach. That will be a perfect spot because it's right around the corner from the kitchen. In the last note, we'll finally have mercy on the poor lady and tell her that it was all a joke. Surely, she'll understand that we're just having some summer fun."

Colin grinned broadly, that glint back in his eye. "Hey, do *you* want to write the last three messages?" he offered graciously.

"I'll leave that up to you," Sam said quickly. "You already know what to write."

"Well, I guess I could let Caleb write the messages," Colin decided. "He was the one who asked Gabriel to bring in the magic kit."

Suddenly, Sam and Colin heard the door handle jiggle and saw the door open. Almost by instinct, they both reacted by jumping in front of the invisible writing on the wall.

Thankfully, while they had been plotting, Jordan had finished writing the last words on the wall. All of their classmates had returned to their seats.

It was truly amazing how innocent they looked, all appearing to be working diligently on their projects. All but Sam and Colin, that is—both of them stood stiffly against the wall with fake smiles plastered on their faces.

Fortunately, Mrs. Benson ignored the boys' odd appearance and zeroed in on the other children, seemingly hard at work.

She stared at them in awe. "I'm so proud of you children," she gushed, resting her hand on her cheek. "And to think I was worried about you getting into trouble while I was gone." She sighed. "I'm going to march right down to the kitchen freezer and get each one of you an ice cream bar. You certainly deserve a treat."

As Mrs. Benson headed out the door, she turned back around one last time to smile lovingly at them before she headed down the hallway.

As Sam guiltily made his way to his seat, he looked around at the other children. They were no longer trying to look innocent but were slumped in their seats, staring at the floor.

And Sam knew at that moment—Mrs. Benson's praise had left the others feeling as lousy and undeserving as he felt.

## Chapter Two
# THE CLEANUP

It was Gabriel who suggested trying to get the ink off of the wall while Mrs. Benson was in the kitchen. He regretted that it was his magic ink that had started the whole thing.

As soon as Gabriel had gotten the words out, all of the kids scrambled across the room to get the bucket from beneath the classroom sink and fill it up with water. Even the kids who normally didn't help out were pitching in to search for sponges or to find the soap—a little praise had done wonders for stirring up their guilty consciences.

As the kids worked feverishly on scrubbing the wall, the thought of Mrs. Benson's return didn't leave their minds for a moment. The only thing that eased their fear was that if she *did* catch them in the act, they knew their teacher would have a hard time figuring out why they were scrubbing a blank wall. In fact, she might even think they were doing a good deed and reward them even more. However, if that happened, they would probably *have* to confess—guilt does have its limits.

After a few minutes, Sam paused from his work and looked over at Colin, who was scrubbing the bottom of the wall. Sweat dripped from his friend's nose, and he had turned a blotchy red. Sam looked around at the other kids, who were working just as feverishly.

Sam couldn't help but think what the scene would look like to an outsider. It would certainly appear they had gone stark raving mad, scrubbing a bare concrete wall for no reason, working as if their lives depended on it. He chuckled out loud at the thought, but was quickly brought back to reality by his classmates' cold, stern glances. He got back to work.

For the next few minutes, the kids did their best to scrub as much of the wall as possible, hoping to erase any remnants of the invisible writing. However, the task wasn't easy—the transparent ink blended in with the paint on the wall, giving no hint of its exact location.

All at once, the children's heart sank when they heard Mrs. Benson outside the door talking to Mrs. Fisher, who normally teaches fifth-grade but had volunteered to teach camp all summer. The kids recognized her voice right away.

They were lucky. Mrs. Fisher had cornered their teacher, anxious to talk about her vacation plans. "North Carolina?" they heard Mrs. Benson's muffled voice say. "Oh, I hear that's beautiful."

As the children raced back to the cabinets to put the bucket and sponges away, they could hear Mrs. Fisher going into great detail about her cabin rental on Lake Lure and her family's plan to go horseback riding in the mountains. An occasional "Really?" or "That sounds wonderful!" could be heard from their kind teacher, who was trying her best to sound thrilled.

In haste, one of the children had poured out the water in the bucket too fast into the sink, and water splashed onto the floor. The children quickly stashed the bucket and sponges in the cabinet and scrambled to their seats just in the nick of time.

When Mrs. Benson opened the door, she was immediately baffled at the sight of a classroom of children perched upright with their hands folded in their laps.

Even though the children *appeared* to be the picture of good behavior, something didn't ring true. As she zoomed in on their faces, flushed pink and sweaty, a puzzled look swept across her face. She slowly looked around. . . .

The room was so quiet that not a whisper could be heard, only the panting of many out-of-breath young children.

Their teacher suddenly noticed the puddle on the floor. Her eyes snapped back to the children, who were beginning to nervously fidget in their seats. Mrs. Benson glared at her students, but they remained quiet.

After a few minutes of silence, she calmly went over to the counter and retrieved a wad of paper towels. She bent down to soak up the water from the floor, while the children remained frozen in their seats.

After she had finished the task, Mrs. Benson didn't say a word in response to their suspicious behavior. She went ahead with her plan to pass out the cold treats—but she did so in an awkward silence that made them wish they could vanish into thin air. . . .

After they had finished eating their treats, the tension in the room had subsided a bit. Mrs. Benson informed the children that she had a special research project for them to do—they were to write about two animals that you could find in a zoo.

Mrs. Benson claimed that the assignment was to prepare them for Mr. Clark's visit the next day, but some kids suspected that it was punishment for their odd behavior.

Whatever the reason, Sam didn't mind the assignment because it would prepare him for his trip to Africa. He spent the rest of the afternoon learning about the hippopotamus and cheetah. He wrote on his paper:

Hippopotamus—a large mammal from swampy areas, lakes, and rivers in Africa, which eats plants, mostly at night, making it nocturnal (active at night). It can stay underwater five to six minutes and weighs up to 10,000 pounds. It has unusual pores on its body that exude a thick, oily, pink sweat—yuck!

Cheetah—the world's fastest land animal, which can travel up to 70 miles per hour. It has a long, slender body, weak jaws, and small teeth and is not an aggressive animal. Its diet consists of gazelles or other small animals. Can live 10 to 15 years. Females live alone. Males live in small groups.

## Chapter Three
## ZOOLOGY CAMP

Sam crept into zoology class the next morning and quietly took a seat by his brother Max, across the table from Colin. He still had knots in his stomach from the day before, afraid their desperate attempt to erase the writing from the wall had failed. He half expected a police car to be parked outside of the school when they arrived and to find out that zoology camp had been cancelled.

Sam hadn't had the heart to tell Max about

the prank. He knew that Max would only work himself into a frenzy about it, worried that he wouldn't get to go to camp—so Sam had suffered all night long, fretting to himself.

When Mr. Clark entered the room at a quarter past nine, he looked rather serious, and Sam slid down in his chair as the man cleared his voice. "Um, class, I have an announcement," he began, looking at all of them rather sternly.

He stood silent for a moment to wait for the chatter to die down. Then he continued, "Some of you may not be able to stay in class today." He frowned and looked at them in silence.

Sam's heart almost stopped, and he was about to jump up to blurt out a confession when Mr. Clark started to speak again. "You may not be able to stay in class today because . . . only the *brave* can stay."

"Huh?" Sam mumbled, drawing attention to himself.

Mr. Clark looked Sam squarely in the eyes and said, "That's right, young man, do you have courage?" His beady eyes glared at him until

Sam finally spoke.

"N-n-not really," Sam stammered, his face turning purple.

To Sam's great relief, Mr. Clark went on, choosing to ignore his clumsy answer. "I'm talking about real courage," Mr. Clark said forcefully, pounding his fist on the desk beside him. "Courage enough to face a four-hundred-pound lion and live to tell about it."

"How about you?" Mr. Clark said, quickly shifting his focus to Max.

Max squirmed in his seat and didn't answer.

"Be prepared, young girls and boys, because we're going to do the next best thing. I've brought to you footage that will make you think that you're doing just that. It is the actual footage of an attack by a lion on a cameraman in the foothills of Africa. Amazingly, the cameraman survived to tell the tale, and the film was recovered during his rescue."

Mr. Clark paused to look at them to gauge their reaction. Then he continued. "Any child who does not wish to view this film should leave the room *now*. Mrs. Fisher would be happy to accommodate you in pottery class."

Mr. Clark's mustache twitched as his eyes scanned the room, pausing to stare at each child intently. "Go on," he urged the faint at heart. "Leave now if you have any doubt."

He waited for a few moments as two girls and a boy skittered out of their seats and fled the room, not bothering to look back.

"All right, I am assuming that the rest of you can stomach what we are about to see," he said in a matter-of-fact way, and with a flick of a switch, he turned on the projector.

If Mr. Clark's intention was to scare them to death, he certainly had succeeded because most of the children covered their eyes as the film began. The others squirmed in their seats.

The film started innocently enough, reciting facts about the lion. However, it was difficult for the children to listen to that part, while worried about the upcoming grisly scene.

At the very end came the much-dreaded vicious attack by the lion. As the children dug their nails into the seats and clamped their eyes shut, they were tormented by the ferocious sounds of the lion mauling its prey. And then, finally, the screen went blank and silent. . . .

The children sat motionless for a few seconds, traumatized by what they had just heard. Knowing that it really happened made it all the more gut-wrenching.

"Just wanted you kids to face the reality of the animal kingdom," Mr. Clark finally said. "We, as zookeepers, have to keep this utmost in our minds every single day as a means of survival. If we get too comfortable with the animals and forget what they are capable of, it could mean our demise."

Mr. Clark, sensing the intensity in the room, shifted to a more light-hearted topic. "Okay, now that you realize the dangers we face as zookeepers, let me share with you the delights we experience as well. For the rest of the morning, we will be discussing the fascinating world of another large African mammal group, the gorillas. Not only are these animals gentle, they are very smart.  After lunch, you will learn about other interesting animals found in a zoo."

Max wrote in his notebook that morning:

Gorillas are large, quiet, gentle apes that live in Africa. They are vegetarians. They have no tails.  Male gorillas are larger than females and are twice as heavy. Males grow a saddle-shaped patch of silver hair on their backs at around 12 years of age. These adult males are called silverbacks. Gorillas rarely drink water because they get the water they need from their food. An average adult male eats around 50 pounds of food a day. Gorillas live in small groups of six or seven, made up of one silver-back, several females, and their young. Gorillas can climb but can't swim. They can live up to 35 years in the wild.

After a couple of hours of studying gorillas,

the zoologist glanced down at his watch, just as a lady wheeled a cart of sack lunches into the room. "Right on time," he said, looking up at her. "I think these kids are as hungry as a bunch of gorillas."

"Mrs. McLean!" Sam blurted out when he recognized her. He kicked Colin under the table to get his attention. "What is *she* doing here? I thought she only cleaned the school at night," Sam whispered.

"Oh, hello," Mrs. McLean said, upon hearing her name. "Mrs. Toby is out sick today, so the school asked if I could fill in."

"Did you clean the school last night?" Colin asked awkwardly.

"As a matter of fact, I did," she said. "But don't worry about me. I got plenty of rest last night before coming in today. I didn't have to clean *all* of the rooms since school is out."

"How about *this* room?" Sam said, turning a chalky white. "Did you clean *this* room?"

"Yes, I did," Mrs. McLean said. "And the strange thing about this room was that there were little squiggly lines that glowed in the dark all over the wall."

"No words?" Colin let slip out.

Sam kicked him hard under the table.

"Ouch!" Colin shouted out.

Mrs. McLean gave Colin a strange look and then mumbled, "Nope, just little lines." She eyed them suspiciously for a moment before turning and wheeling the cart out of the room.

After a few moments, the door opened again, and Mrs. McLean stuck her head inside. Colin and Sam jerked their heads toward her, as the other kids continued to chat.

"Don't worry about the lines," she whispered to them. "I cleaned them up." She winked at the two boys and closed the door again.

Sam and Colin blushed, knowing that Mrs. McLean had discovered their secret.

"At least we managed to clean most of it up. It's a good thing we only wrote on the one wall," Colin said.

"Yeah, or she probably wouldn't have been so forgiving," Sam said, relieved.

## Chapter Four
## AFRICA BOUND

A familiar hum echoed through the cabin of the plane. It was driving Max crazy that he couldn't recognize the words to the song or even see who was singing it. The melody kept drifting through the cabin with no end in sight. It kept repeating over and over again. . . .

Sam was sitting a few rows behind Max and knew exactly where it was coming from. Their mom had played the song for them a hundred times when they were little.

*Deep in the jungle, far and wide*
*Hanging in a tree with no place to hide*
*I spy a butterfly and a chimpanzee*
*I can even see a leopard in the tree . . .*

Finally, Sam couldn't take it anymore. He twisted around and stuck his face out in the aisle to see his little sister sitting a few rows back.

"Sydney, stop! Be quiet," he said as forcefully as he could without shouting. He shot her a dirty look to let her know he meant business.

Somebody has to stop that annoying singing, Sam reasoned to himself. Better me than a stranger.

Sam turned to face forward, struggling to get a glimpse of the back of his mom's head ten rows up. He then counted seven rows up and over to the right to find his dad—his spot was empty. He must have gone to the bathroom, Sam decided.

"I hate flying standby," Sam mumbled out loud.

The Stone family missed their original flight because of heavy traffic and had to fly standby for the next flight. Standby means you have to wait until the regular passengers are boarded before you know if there are any seats left. Sam's definition of flying standby is that you get the leftovers or nothing at all, which means you get scattered seats all over the plane.

Sam vented for a few minutes about the shortcomings of flying standby and then suddenly realized something. . . . There was silence. He turned around and poked his face into the aisle to check on his sister. She was sound asleep.

Little kids look so much cuter when they are asleep, Sam thought, as he looked at his sister, who had just turned three.

A few rows up, Max was at peace. His mind drifted off, thinking about zoology camp and how he loved to learn about animals. He thought about how he'd like to run a zoo himself one day.

All of a sudden, the image of the lion in the

video crept into his mind.  Max shuddered and tried to think of something else.  He decided to get out his notes from camp.  Learning facts about some animals found in Africa might come in handy on their safari.

While Max was retrieving his notebook, Sam was a few rows back reaching into his bag to get the old leather journal that had arrived on their doorstep so mysteriously right before Spring Break.  They had never found out who sent the journal *or* the map that had arrived in a separate box.

Sam removed the two sections of the map from a sleeve in the journal.  He laid them on his tray table, carefully lining up the edges to form one complete map.

He searched the map to find the continent of Africa. . . . Sam found it easily.  He knew it was in the center of the world map.

As Sam stared down at the word "Africa" that marked the continent, he suddenly noticed a bold "S" written above the word.

Sam was stunned.

"What's going on?" he blurted out. First a "W" had appeared in the Cayman Islands, then an "I" in Tahiti, and now an "S".

Sam started to get up to tell his brother about the mysterious "S", but the flight attendant stopped him. "You have to stay seated now. We're getting ready to descend," she said sternly.

Sam gave the attendant a frustrated look.

"Do you need to go to the restroom?" she asked, softening her demeanor.

"No, I just need to tell my brother something *very* important," Sam said seriously.

"Can I give him a message for you?" the lady offered.

"Oh . . . okay," Sam said after a few moments. "Tell him an 'S' has appeared on the map. He's three rows up in the aisle seat."

"Will he know what you're talking about?" the attendant asked, confused.

"Yes, he'll know," Sam answered back.

Sam saw the flight attendant stop at Max's seat and kneel down to talk to him. He waited

for a signal from Max that he understood the message.

Max looked back at his brother and smiled.

"Ladies and gentlemen, we are on our final descent into New York and will be landing shortly," the voice on the loud speaker informed the passengers. "Please place your tray table up and make sure your seatbelt is fastened. If you took any of your carry-on luggage out during the flight, please restow it now. For those of you continuing on to Nairobi, Kenya, you can stay on board in New York. However, if you choose to deplane, you must take your boarding pass with you for verification upon reboarding. The flight to Africa is scheduled to depart at four o'clock."

"Only one flight left to go," Max mumbled excitedly as he put his notes back in his bag.

He could feel the nose of the plane shift downward. While the plane made its gradual descent into New York, Max thought about the mysterious letters on the map and what they could mean.

## Chapter Five
# THE PERKY LADY

The Stone family's sense of time was completely thrown off by the time they touched down in Africa. They had left New York at four o'clock in the afternoon on Saturday and had arrived in Africa thirteen hours later. Instead of being five o'clock in the morning on Sunday, like at home, it was noon in Africa. . . . They had lost seven hours.

Mr. Stone carried Sydney, sound asleep, through the terminal while Max and Sam dragged along behind their mom on the way to the baggage claim area. By the time they had collected their luggage and walked out to the transportation area, a bus marked "Kid's Safari Adventures" pulled up to the curb.

"I guess this bus is for you," Mrs. Stone said, walking toward the dark green bus with a huge giraffe painted on it. "It certainly looks festive," she said, staring at the bold, orange letters that ran across the bus.

As soon as she got the words out, tears began to stream down her face.

Sam didn't like to see his mom cry. "We'll miss you, too, Mom," he said quietly.

The doors to the bus popped open and a perky, blonde lady appeared on the steps of the bus. "Come aboard," she said, waving both of her hands. "We've been waiting for you all morning. Your friends are already at the camp."

"*Friends*?" Max said, looking up at his mom.

"Surprise!" Mrs. Stone yelled out, wiping away her tears and managing a smile. "Your cousin Madison and some of your friends from home are here."

Mr. Stone, beaming with pride, bragged, "Your mom worked hard to get family and friends to join our group to build a new school in a village about an hour from your camp. She did such a great job that you're going to recognize quite a few faces in your group. You guys will have a great time at camp while we work in the village."

Mrs. Stone blushed. "You did a lot to make this trip possible yourself."

"All I did was make a few phone calls to get out of work for a week," Mr. Stone replied bashfully. "I can't take any more credit than that."

Max and Sam liked the sound of their dad being off work for a week. At least for a while, they wouldn't have to worry about his dangerous secret work with the FBI.

"Come aboard, kids. I promise we don't bite," the lady said, trying to hurry them up. "We leave that to the animals around here."

The lady giggled at her own joke as the Stone

family stared silently at her.

Finally, Max and Sam climbed aboard with their bags resting like the humps of a camel on their backs. Mr. and Mrs. Stone tried to follow them, but the lady blocked them.

"Sorry, folks. Read the sign on the bus," the lady said sternly. "This vehicle is for k-i-d-s. You have to say good-bye at the door—there's no crying allowed on the bus, especially from parents. I'm sure you understand. It ruins the atmosphere we're trying to create."

Mr. and Mrs. Stone were speechless.

"After all, that's why you're paying us," the blonde woman continued, "for your kids to have fun. Don't worry—we'll take good care of them. You can pick them up in seven days."

With those words, she shut the door and turned toward the kids. "Are you ready for an adventure?" she shouted out enthusiastically.

Nobody on the bus answered.

"I didn't hear you. Are you ready for an adventure?" the perky lady yelled out again.

"Yes!" they all shouted loudly, hoping they

wouldn't have to repeat their answer.

It worked. The perky bus driver looked thrilled with their response and clapped her hands together. "Now that's the spirit I like to see," she said, before sliding into her seat.

As the bus lurched forward, the driver looked over at Mr. and Mrs. Stone, looking more worried than ever, still standing at the curb. She smiled and shouted at them through the closed door, "Bye. See you in a week."

Max and Sam tried desperately to wave through the small windows, but the lady drove away so quickly that all they managed to do was to put their hands up to the window.

The camp vehicle hadn't even made its way out of the airport terminal when a piercing sound sent shock waves throughout the bus.

"Oh, goodness," they heard the perky lady say. "I don't know why the microphone does that every time I turn it on. Hold on—let me turn the volume down."

The kids clamped their hands over their ears until finally the noise faded away.

"Sorry about that, kids. Didn't mean to break your eardrums," the woman said as she spoke into the microphone. "I am Ms. Sarah, and I will be your safari camp guide for the week. We are heading to camp right now, where you will be required to set up your tent and get your supplies for the week. We have one very important rule here at Kid's Safari Adventures, and this rule is never —"

Ms. Sarah was interrupted by her two-way radio. They heard the microphone click off and saw Ms. Sarah stow it in its holder.

She picked up her radio transmitter just as a man's voice repeated, "What's your location?"

Ms. Sarah answered back, a little annoyed, "I just left the airport. Heading your way."

Their camp guide could then be heard alternating between responses, "Uh-huh . . . yes . . . uh-huh . . . yes."

As the succession of short answers continued, the kids scanned the exciting landscape out their windows as they passed exotic animals grazing in grass fields and gathering around muddy ponds. The landscape was sprinkled with flower-cluster thorn trees.

At last, Ms. Sarah put down her transmitter and turned on the microphone again. The children quickly plugged their ears to block out the horrific squealing.

"Oh, drats," Ms. Sarah said, frazzled by the awful noise herself. "I guess you're thinking you won't make it out of here with your hearing intact. You'll be glad to know we won't be taking this bus on our safari in the morning. The speaker system in the other bus works fine."

Ms. Sarah paused for a moment. "Well, jiminy crickets," she said. "Where was I before I got interrupted by that meddling boss of mine? He just bugs me to death, wanting to know my whereabouts every minute."

Max and Sam giggled under their breath. Their grandma from Kentucky used that same expression, and they thought she was the funniest person in the world. Ms. Sarah was beginning to grow on them already.

"Oh, I remember now," Ms. Sarah said. "I

was going to tell you about the rule that is never to be broken. That rule is—"

Suddenly, Ms. Sarah slammed on the brakes and threw the gearshift in park. The kids almost went flying through the air, but managed to grab the poles lining the aisle to stabilize themselves.

"Would you look at that!" she said, popping out of her seat and peering out the door of the bus. "That's the biggest lion I have ever seen."

Max and Sam couldn't believe their ears. A lion—*free* to roam around? What's wrong with this place?

Hoping Ms. Sarah was playing a joke on them, all five of the passengers ran to the right side of the bus to look out.

There, not ten feet from them, was a gigantic lion sitting lazily on the side of the road. He looked like he didn't have a care in the world.

Ms. Sarah explained to them that lions roam freely in the area because they don't *have* to hide. Other animals hide from them, not the other way around.

Ms. Sarah said that sometimes people pay a high price for giving this animal the freedom it enjoys. "I don't want to scare you," Ms. Sarah said. "But the village to the east of the savanna we will be exploring tomorrow has had five lion attacks in the last year."

The children gulped hard upon hearing this astonishing news.

Ms. Sarah went on to tell them some interesting facts about the lion and why it is so important that other animals have a way to blend in with their surroundings to protect themselves from these fierce predators.

"You'll see that nature has provided many animals a way to camouflage themselves as a means of survival," Ms. Sarah said.

Sam thought back to the invisible ink on the wall and how it had escaped detection. If only we could douse ourselves with some invisible ink, he thought, we might just make it out of this place in one piece.

## Chapter Six
# CAMPOUT

By the time the kids reached camp, they were still reeling about having just seen the most feared predator in Africa. And, understandably, the image of the huge lion sitting casually at the side of the road dampered their desire to leave the safety of the enclosed bus.

"Come on, kids," Ms. Sarah pleaded with them. "The camp is surrounded by a security fence—you'll be safe inside these grounds."

Ms. Sarah's boss, Mr. Wilson, an unfriendly

man with thinning brown hair, came over to see what was going on.

Ms. Sarah stepped outside of the bus and explained to him the reason for the children's reluctance. "We saw an enormous lion sitting on the edge of the plain in clear view," the guide told her hefty boss. "The kids are sort of spooked now." She paused and moved closer to him. "I didn't get a chance to explain the important rule to them," she whispered. "But from the looks of things, enforcing it won't be a problem with these kids. The lion took care of that."

Mr. Wilson, being a no-nonsense kind of man, climbed aboard the bus. His tall frame towered to the ceiling of the bus, and the kids shrunk from his presence. "Off now," he snapped to the children. "It's time to go. No need to worry here," he said, shooing them off like flies.

The children fled the bus, convinced that a lion would be tame compared to Mr. Wilson, who didn't seem to have an ounce of patience.

As soon as Max and Sam had stumbled off the bus and gained their bearings, they saw the familiar faces their mom and dad had promised. Both of them lit up at the sight of friends.

Standing to their left were: Katie and Carissa, the twins, who had been in Max's class last year; Jordan, Tyler, Grady, and Christian, who were boys in Sam's grade at school; and another girl who they didn't recognize. They figured she must be their cousin, Madison, who they hadn't seen in years.

When the boys rushed over, the group buzzed with excitement.

"We saw a giraffe over there," Katie said, pointing to a thorn tree. "It was just standing there, eating leaves."

"And we saw a *gigantic* lion," Max and Sam blurted out at the same time.

"You did? *Where*?" Carissa gasped.

"Right around the corner from here, sitting on the side of the road," Max informed them.

The kids stared at each other, still adjusting to the fact that there were wild animals around every bend.

"We could see if it's still there, if only it didn't break the rule," Jordan said, pretending that he would actually be brave enough to do such a thing.

"Are you crazy?" Christian shrieked.

"What rule?" Max said, anxious to finally get to hear this so-called rule.

"We're not allowed to go outside of the camp fence," Grady informed Max and Sam. "If we do . . . we could get attacked by a wild animal."

Sam flinched at the thought and then, on purpose, changed the subject. "We still have to set up our tent," he said abruptly.

"We'll help you," Katie said. "It's easy."

All of a sudden, a shrill, loud voice called out from the speaker, "Snake alert. Snake alert. A large snake has been spotted in the camping area."

Ms. Sarah's flustered voice repeated the alert over and over again as the children started screaming and running around in circles.

Without any place to go but the tents, which

a snake could easily hide in, the children continued to run around in chaos until they, one by one, collapsed in the dirt. Calming down a bit, the kids formed a circle with their backs together so they could look out for the snake.

"Where is the bathroom?" Sam asked, after a few minutes.

"Huh?" Carissa said, looking over at him.

Sam repeated his question as loud as he could, "Where's the bathroom?"

"It's outside the fence in that building," she yelled back, pointing. "You need a guard to walk you there. Boy, it's sure hard to hear sitting this way."

"At least it's better than our last trip," Max mumbled.

"Huh?" several of the kids said at once.

"It's better than our last trip," Max repeated, almost screaming. "We stayed in Tahiti in a hut and had to use an outhouse."

"A what?" Tyler shouted, turning inward to hear better.

"Let's take turns guarding so we can talk normally," Katie said, turning around with the others.

"Max will guard first," Sam said.

"Me?" Max said, rolling his eyes.

"Oh, I'll do it," Madison volunteered.

"I've got an idea," Max said, relieved to be able to talk normally again. "While we're sitting here, I'll quiz you about the animals of Africa."

"I guess it beats sitting around doing nothing," Sam said. "At least we can kill some time and hope someone catches the snake."

"Don't use the word 'kill' at a time like this," Carissa said seriously.

"I won't be able to get a minute's sleep tonight with that snake slithering around," Katie said, cringing at the thought of a scary snake lurking in the shadows.

"Now we know how the animals must feel, being on the lookout for predators all of the time," Max pointed out.

"Yeah, but who would have guessed *we'd* be the prey?" Madison said grouchily.

## Chapter Seven
# SPOT THE ANIMALS

When the kids climbed aboard the safari bus the next morning, they hadn't had a moment's peace all night long. They had lain awake in the dark terrified that they would be bitten by the elusive snake.

Red-eyed and miserable, they took their seats on the newly arrived bus. Waiting in their seats for the bus to depart, many of the kids closed their eyes for the first time in hours, confident that since the bus hadn't been parked on the premises, it couldn't house the snake.

The children could see Ms. Sarah coming from the campout area carrying a brown canvas bag. She quickly walked over to the bus and climbed the stairs, placing the bag beside the driver's seat before she started the engine.

As they began the bumpy ride away from the campsite, Max and Sam, by habit, clumsily covered their ears when they heard the microphone click on.

They were pleasantly surprised when they heard—not even the least bit of static—only the sound of Ms. Sarah's perkier-than-ever voice. It was obvious that she hadn't been at the campsite to worry about a slimy critter all night long, like they had.

"Kids, I'm so glad to see you again this morning," she chirped. "I hope you are all rested and ready for a fabulous day. As I drive, I'm going to be discussing the animals that you will find on the grassy plains of Africa, or the *savannas* as they are called. Feel free to take notes or ask any questions along the way."

Max slowly lifted up his eyelids and looked out the window. He was annoyed that he was so tired at a time like this. The plains of Africa were so beautiful, already alive with activity. The sun had cast a soft golden light on the grassy fields, and the leaves of the trees, covered in dew, looked like they were shimmering with sparkles of light.

Ms. Sarah continued with her lesson on the animals of the savanna, not bothering to slow down to accommodate the half-alert children.

"The savanna of Africa is home to some of the largest, fastest, tallest, and most unusual animals in the world!" Ms. Sarah boasted, proud of her adopted land. "Yes, it's true . . . a savanna can be a danger zone, especially to the animals that must live and survive there. And for that reason alone, we will be viewing the animals from the safety of the bus."

The kids certainly didn't want to argue against staying in the sanctuary of the bus. It sounded like a good plan to them.

Ms. Sarah added, "But don't worry about not

being able to see the animals—we'll fold the top of the bus down after lunch to give you an incredible view."

Sam was glad to hear that. He thought wind in his face was just what he needed to wake up.

"Now, let's go over some of the animals that call the wide-open grassland their home," Ms. Sarah said as energetically as ever. "Let's first start with one of the most feared animals, the lion. Now I know some of you that came in yesterday have already heard this information, but please bear with me while I go over these facts again with the other children."

Max, now as awake as he could be after a sleepless night compounded by jetlag, was more than happy to hear the information again. He thought lions were the most fascinating creatures on earth.

Ms. Sarah pulled over to the side of the road to find her notes about the lion. As she did, Max thought back to the image of the huge lion casually lying in the grass beside the road.

Finally, their tour guide started to read.

A lion's roar can be heard up to five miles away. A lion may roar to protect its pride, or family, from other animals invading its territory. A male lion will sometimes fight until death to protect its territory. The female lions or lionesses usually do the hunting, sometimes in pairs. A lion can drag a 660 pound zebra by itself, a task that would normally take six humans to do. Even though the female lions catch the food, the male lions usually eat first.

Ms. Sarah broke away from her notepad and stood up to face the kids, still with a microphone in her hand. "There is a good chance that we might run across a herd of zebras during our seven-day journey because they are always on the move looking for grass to eat and water to drink. While we're pulled over, let's go over some facts about the zebra."

Ms. Sarah thumbed through her notebook for a few moments until she found the right page.

Then she began to read:

The male leader, or stallion, is the head of a family group of zebras. The family group is made up of the stallion, several females, and their young. It is a good thing that zebras are constantly moving, because they are prime hunting prey for lions and hyenas.

When Ms. Sarah was finished reading, she looked up.

"Ms. Sarah," Katie called out. "Don't their stripes make them stand out and be more vulnerable to attacks?"

"Great question!" Ms. Sarah said, pointing at Katie. "You would think that the black-and-white stripes of a zebra would make it more visible to a predator. Amazingly, though, the stripes actually help *hide* the zebra rather than make it more visible. When the zebra is moving, its black-and-white stripes blur the vision of its predator, and this confuses it."

Ms. Sarah paused for more questions and then continued. "We might also run into a rhinoceros or two on our expedition, grazing in the grass. The ones you see here have two horns and are usually gray in color. These animals are powerful enough to overturn a vehicle."

"Has that ever happened?" Jordan asked.

"Not *yet*," Ms. Sarah said teasingly before she climbed back into the driver's seat.

Once the bus started rolling again and bouncing the kids from side to side, Sam wished they could pull over again. It was much easier to concentrate on what was being said without being jerked around.

Ms. Sarah ignored the bumps and clicked on the microphone. "We will more than likely run across elephants and giraffes today. The African elephant is the heaviest and the second-tallest land animal in the world. It stands nearly thirteen feet tall and can consume two hundred pounds of grass, berries, bark, twigs, and other plant material in one day."

Ms. Sarah pulled over again to retrieve her binoculars. After a few moments, she said, "Yep, the elephants are there again today. It must be their main stomping ground. Get it? *Stomping*—elephants? How I ever come up with these things, I don't know."

Ms. Sarah seemed quite pleased with herself and giggled in the microphone for at least a full minute before inviting the kids to come up and take turns using the binoculars to view the herd of elephants across the plain.

Ms. Sarah used this time to educate them about the elephant. "Pay close attention to the elephant's long, muscular trunk," she coached them. "It acts like a hand, bringing food or spraying water into its mouth. The elephant also has nostrils at the end of its trunk, so it can smell food or water from miles away."

"Do elephants live with their families?" Tyler asked.

"Yes, they do live in a family group, or herd, which is led by an older female. The family consists of female elephants, called cows, and their young, called calves. Male elephants are called bulls and usually leave the family group at age fourteen to live alone."

"Are elephants smart?" Christian asked.

"They sure are," Ms. Sarah answered. "They have the biggest brain of all land animals and are capable of remembering things for long periods of time."

"There are so many of them," Jordan said, after having his turn at the binoculars. "And most of them look so old."

"That's because many of them *are* old," Ms. Sarah explained. "Elephants can live to be seventy years old. And you usually see them traveling in large groups of twenty to thirty."

After all of the kids had used the binoculars, Ms. Sarah was eager to go. "Okay, children, take your seats. We have places to go and animals to see. We have a lot of *grassy* ground to cover."

Ms. Sarah chuckled for a few moments until she spied a beautiful herd of zebras gracefully galloping across the plain. "Children, look!"

she shouted out.

After Max had stared at the zebras for a few seconds, his vision went fuzzy, and he could understand what Ms. Sarah meant about the stripes helping the zebras confuse predators.

"Ms. Sarah," Grady called out. "Do all of the zebras have the *same* stripes?"

"No, they don't," Ms. Sarah answered. "Every zebra has a different pattern of stripes. It helps them to tell each other apart."

Ms. Sarah started the engine. She drove a little bit farther down the road and discovered a giraffe eating leaves from an acacia tree. She pulled over and explained to them, "The giraffe's long eighteen-inch tongue is coated with mucus to protect it from the thorns of the acacia tree."

While Ms. Sarah leafed through her notepad to find her notes about the giraffe, the children watched this soaring animal eat its mid-morning snack.

This untamed part of Africa, with high grass and unkept fields, seemed like a wide-open zoo.

It catered more to animals than people.

The children heard the microphone click back on, and Ms. Sarah began to read her notes:

The giraffe is the world's tallest animal. It can be as tall as 19 feet, with its neck alone being six feet long. The long neck helps them watch for predators. These amazing animals can run 35 miles an hour, which is faster than a racehorse. The ones you will see here have brown and cream patches shaped like triangles. Giraffes get their water from the leaves they eat, so they don't drink from the rivers or ponds very often. This is a good thing because when giraffes drink from a body of water, they have to slide their front legs apart and put their heads down. Lions usually attack giraffes when their heads are down.

Ms. Sarah pulled the bus back onto the

bumpy road and announced, "For the rest of our ride this morning, we will be talking about some unusual insects found in Africa. A trip here wouldn't be complete without learning about them."

Ms. Sarah started off by telling the children about the large tsetse fly, which has a very painful bite and can cause a horrible sleeping sickness. Then, the children gasped in horror as she told them about the assassin bug that prowls the forest looking for a victim.

"It pierces the skin and injects a substance that turns the inside of the victim's body into soup," Ms. Sarah said matter-of-factly. "Then the bug drinks the soup using its mouth as a straw."

"Ooh!" the children moaned, not believing that a bug so terrible could exist.

Max and Sam thought these bugs sounded more dangerous than any ferocious animal.

Ms. Sarah went on to tell them that Africa is also home to the goliath beetle, the heaviest insect in the world. "It is the size of an apple, believe it or not, and can still fly," she said.

All of a sudden, their guide let out a shriek. "Look!" she said, pointing at a speeding blur of an animal in the distance. "There's a cheetah—the fastest land animal there is! It can run up to seventy miles per hour. Do you realize what a treat it is to spot one of those?" Ms. Sarah chuckled out loud. "No pun intended of course—get it—*spot* a cheetah—a cheetah has spots!"

Ms. Sarah was still chuckling when the bus's engine made a rattling noise and died.

"Rats!" Ms. Sarah yelled out. "This old bus gives me so much trouble." She shook the steering wheel in frustration. "Children, stay in here while I have a look at the engine—believe it or not, I am an excellent mechanic. Around here, it comes with the job description. That's why I always bring my bag of tools."

Ms. Sarah grabbed the bag beside her seat and stormed out of the bus into the blazing sun, all the while huffing under her breath. She lifted up the hood of the bus and poked around in the engine.

Some of the kids started talking in groups, while others continued to scan the fascinating landscape. Then a chilling cry, coming from outside of the bus, halted all activity.

The children jumped out of their seats and raced to the front of the bus, timidly peeking out the windshield. . . .

They couldn't see Ms. Sarah anywhere.

"Oh, no!" screamed Madison. "The cheetah must have gotten Ms. Sarah."

The children then heard groaning sounds coming from the area of the still-open hood of the bus.

"Somebody needs to go check on Ms. Sarah. Maybe she needs help!" Sam said.

They all stared at each other, hoping some-body would volunteer.

Finally, the thought of Ms. Sarah lying on the ground, hurt, overwhelmed Max. He opened the door of the bus and cautiously climbed down the stairs. Some of the others followed him, cowering behind him as he walked.

Max shivered as he took one careful step at a

time. Slowly, he walked around the corner of the bus and could see Ms. Sarah on the ground.

Max froze and covered his face in horror. The others slowly made their way around the corner and cried out in terror when they saw their perky tour guide stretched out in the dirt.

As their wails echoed across the savanna, animals were alerted for miles.

Suddenly, Max thought he caught a glimpse of something slithering away in the grass on the side of the road. He quit screaming to take a closer look.

Dark in color, the thing looked six feet long.

Could a snake be that long?

*Nah*, Max finally decided—his mind was playing tricks on him. After all, he hadn't had a good night's sleep in days.

## Chapter Eight
# CHARGER

Ms. Sarah was lying totally still on the ground. For a moment, the kids thought she had suffered a heart attack. There was no sign of an animal around, not even a speck of blood. The only thing near her was the open brown bag that she had carried out of the bus.

The kids were just about to check for breathing when Ms. Sarah's eyes fluttered open.

She grasped her ankle and managed to yelp, "I need help fast. I've been bitten by a black mamba!  Stay away from the bag. . . ."

Ms. Sarah collapsed, losing consciousness again.

Max ran back to the bus and spotted the radio transmitter on the driver's seat.  He mumbled to the others what had happened as he nervously tried to decipher the controls of the two-way radio.

As soon as Jordan heard what had happened, he yelled out in horror.  "My dad told me that the black mamba is one of the most venomous snakes in the world!"

Upon hearing this, Max began to panic even more.  "Does anyone know how to work this thing?" he said, holding up the device.

They all shrugged their shoulders.

Sam finally grabbed the transmitter out of Max's hand, pressed a button, and yelled, "Help, somebody.  Does anybody read me?"

He pressed the button again.  "Ms. Sarah has been bitten by a snake," he yelled.  "Help . . . we're miles from camp."

There was no answer.

"I bet the radio quit working when the bus died," Katie said quietly.

Sam glanced up and spotted the herd of elephants in the distance.

"Maybe we can use one of the elephants to carry Ms. Sarah to the village she told us about to get help," he suggested.

"Oh, yeah, and let's go join a circus while we're at it," Max said sarcastically.

All at once, Sam darted off the bus and ran across the vast, dusty plain toward the elephants.

One of the elephants saw Sam coming and lifted her trunk high up in the air . . . then sniffed . . . then trumpeted a long thunderous blast toward the approaching stranger.

Sam ignored the warning and kept charging ahead toward the herd of elephants.

Max knew that this was the last thing his brother should be doing. He jumped off of the bus and chased after Sam.

"Stop!" Max cried out. "Slow down—you're scaring the elephants."

It was too late. . . . The elephant leader viewed Sam as a threat. She puffed out another loud blast, rolled down her trunk, threw back her ears, lowered her head, and charged at Sam.

The ground shook as the powerful animal sped toward him.

Sam panicked at the sight of a huge eight-thousand-pound elephant racing toward him. He stopped running, screamed, and covered his

face in despair.

Sam fell to the ground, trembling with fear. As he lay there, he knew that at any moment the elephant could trample him. He felt like he was on a track waiting to be run over by a train.

Sam's eyes were shut so tightly and he was so consumed with fear, that it took him a few seconds to notice that the ground had stopped shaking.

He slowly lifted up his head and opened his eyes. . . .

Standing in front of him was the biggest animal that he had ever seen.

Frightened, Sam bolted to his feet.

The oversized animal must have sensed that Sam was scared because she slowly reached out her trunk toward him.

Sam laughed nervously at this kind gesture and gently patted the elephant's trunk.

"Thank you for not running over me . . . Charger," Sam said, nicknaming his new animal friend.

Without warning, the elephant suddenly

grabbed Sam by its trunk and whisked him high into the air. Sam somersaulted awkwardly and landed on the broad back of the elephant.

"Whoa!" Sam belted out. "That was scary."

"Come on!" Sam yelled down to Max, who had caught up and was standing below them in shock. "Get on!"

Max was terrified, having seen Sam snatched up and tossed around like a ball. He slowly walked up to the elephant and closed his eyes.

He cringed as the elephant raised him high into the air with her trunk and placed him on the top of her head.

Max opened his eyes and tried not to look down as he scooted back toward Sam.

Max and Sam tried to nudge Charger toward Ms. Sarah, still lying on the ground in the distance, but their large animal friend stayed put.

Sam finally scooted to the head of the elephant and climbed onto its long, strong trunk. The elephant lowered Sam to the ground.

Sam grabbed the end of Charger's trunk as if it were a hand and led her across the dusty grassland toward Ms. Sarah.

When they reached her, Charger seemed to know exactly what to do. The animal gently picked up the wounded lady with her trunk and slowly lifted her.

Max quickly scooted back as far as he could to make room for Ms. Sarah. The elephant carefully placed her on its back. She lay there motionless in a sea of gray, stretched out across the elephant's wide back.

Katie and Carissa couldn't believe their eyes.

They stood outside the bus and gasped as Sam led Charger across the plain in the direction of the village that Ms. Sarah had told them about.

A few minutes into the slow, bumpy ride, Max spotted little mud buildings with straw roofs lined up in a row.

"The village!" Max shouted, pointing at the small buildings in the distance.

After they made their way across the plain of wild grass, Sam led Charger into the village and stopped at the first row of huts.

Max carefully crawled over Ms. Sarah to get to the elephant's head. He then climbed onto Charger's trunk.

The elephant lowered its long, gray trunk to let him down.

Max and Sam spotted a villager peeking out of a building.

Max ran up to him and took his hand. "Please help us. We need help," he said.

The man stared at Max as if he didn't understand. Max led him over to the elephant and pointed up to Ms. Sarah, stretched out on the blanket of gray.

Sam tried to make the man understand. He took his hand and imitated the slithering motion of a snake. He then gathered the tips of his fingers together and imitated a snake biting.

Max tried to help. He looked at the man and said, "Black mamba bit her."

Max and Sam suddenly noticed a spark of recognition in the man's eyes. He got a frightened look on his face and bolted toward one of the little huts. A couple of minutes later, he came back with two other men carrying an old, wooden ladder.

One of them climbed to the top of the elephant's broad back and slid Ms. Sarah down the animal's side to the arms of the other man. They hurriedly carried her into one of the huts.

Max remembered the other kids in their group and turned to Sam. "We need to go back to get the others."

They walked over to Charger's trunk and were lifted up one at a time onto her back. The elephant then turned around and trotted toward its home across the plain.

Sam enjoyed the air tickling the back of his neck as he rested on top of the gently marching elephant. He could relax now that they had gotten Ms. Sarah to safety.

Max's eyes roamed across the field of high grass and feasted on the natural scenery. He smiled when he spotted a majestic eagle soaring above them. Max reached his hand up in the air, feeling like he was flying through the sky himself.

From the vantage point on Charger's back, the boys could spot things they never could on the ground. They saw a cheetah mother and her cubs stretched out in the tall grass.

Amazingly, neither Max or Sam felt afraid. They felt privileged to be able to spy on the animal kingdom from the safety of Charger's back.

This is the life, Sam thought to himself as he looked out over the dusty plain. He knew he was getting to witness things that few other kids ever would.

## Chapter Nine
# CRIES IN THE JUNGLE

As they approached the bus, the boys could see the herd of elephants in the distance. They were behaving differently than before, running around wildly in distress.

Charger raced toward them.

When the group's leader had returned, the elephants stampeded across the plain, stopping near the edge of what looked like a jungle. Max and Sam could hear the unmistakable cries of an elephant coming from deep within the forest.

Charger blasted a loud trumpet sound with her trunk as if she were calling out to the elephant inside the forest.

The jungle looked eerily dark inside. The trees were crammed together so tightly that the sunlight hardly peeked through the dense leaves. Wild calls and hoots from animals inside could be heard.

"What would an elephant be doing inside the forest?" Max asked, bewildered.

"I don't know, but the elephant in the forest must be a member of Charger's family—a part of her herd," Sam said, amazed at the loyalty these larger-than-life animals were demonstrating.

The boys hated seeing Charger so troubled. Against their better judgment, they decided to help their new friend. . . .

As the brothers started to tread through the noisy jungle, they were too scared to speak.

Suddenly, they saw something move in a tree up ahead. They crept closer, holding their breath with fear. Finally, a little brown-faced chimp poked its head through some branches and stared at them. Knowing the boys were watching, he swung from branch to branch, putting on a show for them. He orchestrated his movements with playful grunts as if he were a stage performer.

Max and Sam laughed at this little chimp's playful personality.

All at once, the performance was interrupted by a strange shriek in the distance. The little chimp froze when he heard the frightening sound. Oddly, a big, toothy grin appeared on his face.

Baffled by the chimp's mixed signals, Max and Sam watched him closely.

They heard the strange noise again followed by more odd sounds: a loud moan, a whoop, and then what sounded like a chilling laugh.

"What could that be?" Sam asked, the hair standing up on his neck.

Max watched the chimp scamper high up in the tree until he disappeared from sight.

The boys could hear leaves crunching around them and branches snapping above them as the chorus of odd noises grew—the strange sounds were creating a frenzy around them.

The crazy laugh was getting closer now, and Max and Sam started to panic. They wished they, too, could climb a tree to escape, but the branches surrounding them were too high to reach.

They heard another whoop that seemed to come from right behind them. Max and Sam whirled around and were within arm's reach of a large hyena!

They had learned in camp that hyenas normally travel in a clan. They were right . . . two more hyenas appeared.

Slowly, one of the hyenas started walking toward them.

Just at that moment, a powerful roar thundered through the woods, warning the animals that a fierce predator was close by.

The hyenas quickly scampered away.

Max and Sam were so scared they didn't know which way to run. They stood frozen until the elephant in the jungle cried out again.

They both ran in the direction of the sound of the elephant and kept running until they could see a gray object appearing through the trees.

When they got closer to the elephant, they could hear voices. Max and Sam hid behind some thick bushes to listen.

They couldn't believe what they saw through the window of brush—cages and cages of wild animals. They spotted a baby elephant in an iron-barred cage on the end.

The men who guarded the cages were not African at all. They spoke English. Max and Sam listened as the two men spoke to each other in a heavy British-sounding accent.

One of them, a tall, muscular man with a dark beard, spoke excitedly. "Our catch today will fetch a very high price. We were lucky to find a baby elephant as young as this one. We'll get twice the normal price for a baby like this!"

The other man, wearing thick-rimmed glasses below a bald head, patted the tall man on the back. "Good idea, coming here to catch these wild beasts. I bet the African authorities never police these jungles. They're probably afraid of what might reach out and bite them!"

The men exploded with laughter.

"What are we going to do?" Sam whispered to Max, feeling helpless. "We don't have the strength to go up against these men to free the elephant, and I'm not sure we can survive a trip back through the jungle."

The boys huddled together, trying to disappear in the thick vegetation of the forest.

Just when Max and Sam thought it couldn't get any worse, a loud roar erupted again—only this time it sounded closer than ever. The two boys glared at each other. They were consumed with fear.

All of a sudden, Max and Sam heard the men scream.

Through the bushes, they could see the shaggy mane of a lion's head. The lion was moving slowly toward the two men.

The men backed up as far as they could, their backs pressed against the side of a large, empty cage. The lion moved closer to them, licking his chops.

The men had no choice but to quickly scoot around the corner of the cage and dash into the cage's open door. The men slammed the door shut just as the lion lunged after them.

One of the men, feeling confident the lion couldn't get to them, mocked the huge cat. "Come and get me, you big bully. See if you like the taste of iron bars for dinner."

The lion roared at them, showing a full set of pointed, sharp teeth. After a few attempts at gnawing through the iron bars, the lion lost interest and wandered off.

Max and Sam stayed put for fear of the lion's return. The two animal poachers tried to exit their cage but made a horrifying discovery— they were locked in. They shook the metal bars of the gate violently, trying to force it open. When that didn't work, they tried to put their arms through the narrow bars to reach the ring of keys hanging on a nail attached to a near-by tree.

"It was your idea to install automatic locks on the cages," the muscular man yelled out in rage.

"I was scared we'd forget to lock the cages and the animals would escape," the other one whined with regret.

After a few moments, Sam gained enough courage and leaped out of the bushes, running toward the ring of keys. In a flash, he had opened the baby elephant's cage, and the over-joyed animal came barreling out.

Sam remembered how safe it felt to be sitting on the top of an elephant. He ran over to the animal and grabbed its trunk. The baby elephant scooped him up with his trunk and tossed him onto his back.

Max darted toward the elephant, and the elephant scooped him up, too.

The men pleaded with the boys to let them out of the cage. Max yelled over to them as the elephant started to move away, "Now *you* know how it feels to be locked up in a cage. Don't worry. We'll be sending the police back to free the other animals and lock you up in a permanent cage—called jail."

It wasn't long until the elephant was running at full speed. He charged toward the sound of the other elephants still gathered at the edge of the jungle.

Through the dark forest, the young elephant darted through the thick brush and vines, knocking down everything in its path. Max and Sam yelped as they saw trees being uprooted and plunging to the ground. They dodged this branch and then another as they sped through the jungle toward the plain.

All of a sudden, they were face to face with a spotted leopard, sitting on a low branch of a tree. Its face flashed before them and was gone in an instant before Max and Sam could scream.

The boys caught glimpses of noisy monkeys and birds sitting high up in the trees. These animals hooted and chirped at them as they streaked past them.

Many other animals blending in with the foliage  were a blur to them as they sped by, until they passed a mandrill, the most unusual-looking, colorful animal they had ever seen. Looking as though its face was coated in war paint, the mandrill's bright red nose and sky-blue cheeks stood out as a stark contrast to the greens and browns of the jungle.

Finally, the elephant burst out of the forest and onto the grassland where his family waited for him.  The herd of elephants danced around in a circle to celebrate the return of their young one.  Charger lovingly nudged the baby elephant with her trunk.

Max and Sam took turns scooting onto the baby elephant's head and sliding down his trunk.  Once both of them were safely on the ground, they looked across the plain and could see the broken-down bus in the distance.  Max and Sam walked across the field toward the bus with Charger following close behind them.

"It seems a lot safer with you by our side, Charger," Max yelled back to her.

When they got to the bus, Max and Sam spotted a note stuck on the window. Sam reached for it and read it out loud:

Max and Sam,

Mr. Wilson sent a search party out looking for us when Ms. Sarah didn't answer her radio. They found us and are taking us back to camp. They are still looking for you. If you get this note, stay in the bus until they come back for you. Mr. Wilson said it's too dangerous for you to be wandering around on your own.

Katie and Carissa

P.S. We told a man in the search party that you took Ms. Sarah to the village across the plain. He radioed there and talked to the village doctor who treated Ms. Sarah. She's going to be fine, thanks to you guys.

As Max and Sam waited on the bus, Charger stayed outside, guarding over them. The big elephant had become quite protective of them.

With time on their hands, the two boys began to worry how their parents were going to take the news they had gone into the jungle alone.

"How does this sound?" Sam said, deciding to rehearse their story. "The jungle wasn't *that* bad, Mom and Dad. . . . A chimpanzee performed a circus act for us right before we ran across a clan of hyenas. After that, we were within a few feet of a ferocious lion. Then we rescued a baby elephant from some evil animal kidnappers and charged through the forest knocking over everything in our path. While speeding through the forest, we came face to face with a leopard sitting on a branch of a tree!"

"And then I'll say to them," Max joined in. "We now know that the jungle is a noisy . . . gut-wrenching . . . crazy-like . . . fascinating place that we don't ever want to go in again— the animals can have the jungle all to themselves!"

"They'll probably ground us for life," Sam said, shrugging his shoulders.

"Probably," Max said with a huge grin.

# MAX AND SAM'S SCIENCE PICK
## Making Invisible Ink

Did you know there is a science for writing hidden messages? It is called steganography. One of the ways to hide a message is to write it in invisible ink. There are several ways you can make invisible ink. Here are two:

### Method 1

**Supplies needed**: lemon juice, small glass, toothpick or cotton swab, paper, and iron

**Instructions**: First pour lemon juice in the glass. Soften the point of the toothpick in the juice. Then write the message using the toothpick or cotton swab dipped in juice. Get an adult to iron your paper. The message should appear in brown.

### Method 2

**Supplies needed**: baking soda, water, small glass, toothpick, paper, grape juice, and a heat source

**Instructions**: Mix equal parts of water and baking soda. Dab the toothpick in the mixture and write your message. Read it by holding the paper up to a heat source, such as a light bulb. Paint over the ink on the paper with grape juice to make it a different color.

## NOW THAT'S COOL SCIENCE!